Katie and the British Artists

James Mayhew

ORCHARD BOOKS

For Gabriel Benedict Giacomo Mayhew
— another great British artist —

Thank you for helping with the illustrations!

Thanks to Ben Copperwheat for lending his name,
to Storm and Roxy for helping with Rex,
and the team at Orchard for
always believing in Katie.

ORCHARD BOOKS
338 Euston Road, London NW1 3BH
Orchard Books Australia
Level 17/207 Kent Street, Sydney, NSW 2000
First published in 2008 by Orchard Books
First published in paperback in 2009
ISBN 978 1 84616 737 9
Text and illustrations (except pages 17 and 18) © James Mayhew 2008
Background illustration detail on pages 17 and 18 © Gabriel Mayhew 2008
The right of James Mayhew to be identified as
the author and illustrator of this work has been asserted
by him in accordance with the Copyright,
Designs and Patents Act, 1988.
A CIP catalogue record for this book is available
from the British Library.
1 3 5 7 9 10 8 6 4 2
Printed in China
Orchard Books is a division of Hachette Children's Books, an Hachette Livre UK company.

Katie was off on a trip to the gallery with Grandma.
There were lots of people hurrying past.

"Is everyone going to the gallery?" asked Katie.

"No, they're going to work," said Grandma. "They all
have jobs to do."

"I wonder what job I'll do when I grow up?" thought Katie.

By the time they reached the gallery, Grandma was tired.
"Dear me, what a long walk!" she said, resting on a seat.
"You have a look around. I'll just have a quick snooze."
So Katie looked at the pictures.

She particularly liked a painting
of a shepherd boy and some sheep
called *The Cornfield* by John Constable.

"He's got a great job," said Katie.
"I'd love to be a shepherd."

To her surprise, the boy spoke.

"It's jolly hard work," he said.
"You should try it!"

"All right," said Katie, climbing
over the frame and into
the picture, "I will!"

"I'm Ben Copperwheat," said the boy,
"and that's Rex, my dog."

"Hello, I'm Katie," said Katie.

"Well, come on, Katie, help me with these sheep,"
said Ben. "They're wandering off in all directions!"

It was hot, dusty work, but eventually Katie, Ben and Rex herded the sheep safely into the meadow.

"Phew!" said Katie. "I'm puffed out!"
"I have to do this every day," said Ben.
"You could try a different job," suggested Katie.
"Let's look in the gallery for ideas!"

Katie took Ben and Rex into the gallery. Ben saw a picture called
Rain, Steam and Speed by J.M.W Turner.

"How exciting!" said Ben. "I could be a train driver."

"Come on, then," said Katie, and they climbed inside the picture.

The train was puffing across a bridge,
but when the driver saw Katie and Ben waving,
he stopped the train.

"Please can we drive the train?" asked Katie.

"Well, I could use some help," said the driver. "All aboard!"

Ben helped to drive the train, while Katie shovelled coal.
The train went faster and faster, lickety-split along the track.
The ladies' bonnets blew away and the gentlemen lost their hats!

"Slow down!" yelled the passengers.
"Faster!" shouted Katie and Ben.
Clickety-clack went the train!

Suddenly, there was a *BANG!* The train slowly ground to a halt.

"Oh, dear," said Katie. "Is it broken?"

"We've blown a valve," said the driver, grabbing a spanner. "It will take ages to mend. You'd better hop off before you do any more damage!"

"I don't think I should be a train driver after all," said Ben, as they walked back to the frame and climbed into the gallery.

"Look at that horse!" said Ben. He was pointing at a painting called *Whistlejacket* by George Stubbs.

"Perhaps you could be a horseman with the Royal Guard," said Katie.

"I'd love that!" said Ben, so they quickly climbed inside.

Ben hopped up onto Whistlejacket.
"There's nowhere to ride in this picture," he said.
Katie fumbled in her pocket and found a few old
crayons. She quickly drew some hills and fields.
"Perfect," said Ben, galloping off.

"Woah! Steady!" said Ben, but
Whistlejacket was hard to control.
Ben was flung up into the air . . .

and landed on a hill covered in soft
flowers that Katie had drawn.

"Oof!" he gasped. "Perhaps I'm
not very good at riding either."
So they left Whistlejacket to gallop
around his new world and jumped
into the gallery.

"I still don't know what job would be best for me," sighed Ben.

"You could become a painter – like Papa!" said a little girl from a picture. It was called *The Painter's Daughters Chasing a Butterfly* by Thomas Gainsborough.

"Come and see!" said the girl's sister. So Ben and Katie climbed inside.

The girls showed Ben their father's paintings.
They were nearly all portraits of them.
"You could try to paint us as well!" suggested the girls.
"I don't know how to paint," said Ben.
"Here, have my crayons," said Katie. "Try drawing instead!"

Ben tried to draw the girls as they chased butterflies, but he found it very hard.

"It's no good," he said. "I don't think I could be an artist either!"

"Never mind," giggled the girls. "Come and chase butterflies with us – it's fun!"

Ben was rather good at catching butterflies with his hat.

"But I can't do that for a job . . . can I?" he asked.

"Well," said the girls, "you could be an explorer and discover rare insects and birds . . . "

"I could sail around the world, to faraway islands!" said Ben.

"And I know where to find a ship!" said Katie. "Come on!"

They said goodbye to the girls and jumped into the gallery,
where Katie showed Ben a painting of a ship called
The Fighting Temeraire by J.M.W Turner.

"That's perfect for an adventure!" said Ben, as they climbed
through the frame.

It was evening in the painting, and the sun
was slowly setting over the sea.
Katie saw a rowing boat tied to a jetty.
"Let's row out to the big ship," she said.

When they reached the ship, they climbed aboard. It was a very old ship that no one used any more, so they had it all to themselves.

"Ahoy there!" shouted Katie, climbing the rigging. "Shiver me timbers!"

"Hoist the mainsail!" laughed Ben from the deck.

They explored all over the ship, but then
Ben heard distant sounds drifting across the
sea from the gallery.

"I'd know that sound anywhere," he said.
"It's my sheep! I must go and find them!"

"It sounds like your sheep are calling for you," said Katie, as they rowed back to the picture frame.

"Perhaps I left the gate open . . ." said Ben.

In the gallery, they found Ben's sheep waiting.

"I must get them home before dark," he said.

Ben whistled to Rex and together they rounded up the sheep, quickly and neatly, in front of the cornfield picture.

"In you go," Ben said. And he counted them in, one by one.

"I think you've found your perfect job!" said Katie.

"You're right! I love being a shepherd after all . . ." said Ben. He gave Katie her crayons back. "And I think *you* should be an artist. Perhaps one day you'll have a painting in the gallery!"

"Perhaps one day I will . . ." said Katie, waving goodbye.

Katie found Grandma still snoozing on the seat.

"How can you sleep when the gallery is so exciting?" said Katie. "You don't know what you're missing!"

"Well, you know what they say about counting sheep," said Grandma. "And how it helps you fall asleep . . . "

"Grandma!" said Katie. "Did you . . . ?"

"Did I see any sheep?" asked Grandma, smiling. "Now that would be telling, wouldn't it!"

 # More about British Art

Many of the most famous artists were Italian, French or Spanish, but in the 18th and 19th centuries, British artists began to prove they were just as talented and brilliant. The four artists in this story were most famous for painting spectacular scenes or landscapes.

JOHN CONSTABLE (1776-1837)

John Constable was born in a tiny village called East Bergholt, Suffolk. He was a great landscape painter and sketched many studies of trees and skies before starting work on his huge paintings. He is so famous that the places he painted in Suffolk – which exist almost unchanged to this day – are known as 'Constable Country'. It is still possible to visit the very place where *The Cornfield* was painted.

THOMAS GAINSBOROUGH (1727-1788)

Thomas Gainsborough was born in Sudbury, Suffolk, and many of his pictures show local countryside scenes. He was also a skilful portrait painter, as demonstrated in *The Painter's Daughters Chasing a Butterfly*, and he even went on to paint pictures of the royal family.

GEORGE STUBBS (1724-1806)

George Stubbs was born in Liverpool and was especially famous for painting horses. With *Whistlejacket*, he decided not to include any landscape in the background at all, so the viewer would really look in detail at his magnificent horse.

J.M.W. TURNER (1775-1851)

Joseph Mallord William Turner was born in Covent Garden, London. His pictures were often experimental, showing different ways of painting dramatic weather and skies. Turner even went sketching on trains and ships to learn how to paint movement and light. He especially liked storms and sunsets, often over the sea.

Rain, Steam and Speed surprised many people when it was first exhibited because it was so different to anything they'd seen before. The earliest steam trains often had open-top carriages and at the time people thought they were very strange-looking and modern.

In *The Fighting Temeraire Tugged to Her Last Berth to be Broken Up* we see a famous old wooden battleship being pulled by a small modern tugboat. The ship had become 'old-fashioned' and no one wanted it any more, so it was broken up for scrap. The painting is about how things change with time. Turner makes the picture look beautiful, but a little sad, with his fantastic sunset.

All these paintings are in The National Gallery, London. It is free to go and see them – and many others by these great British artists. What are you waiting for?

Acknowledgements:

The Cornfield, 1826 (oil on canvas), Constable, John (1776-1837)/National Gallery, London, UK/The Bridgeman Art Library; Rain, Steam and Speed, The Great Western Railway, painted before 1844 (oil on canvas), Turner, Joseph Mallord William (1775-1851)/National Gallery, London, UK/The Bridgeman Art Library; Whistlejacket, 1762, Stubbs, George (1724-1806)/National Gallery, London, UK/The Bridgeman Art Library; The Painter's Daughters Chasing a Butterfly, c.1759, Gainsborough, Thomas (1727-1788)/National Gallery, London, UK/The Bridgeman Art Library; The Fighting Temeraire Tugged to Her Last Berth to be Broken Up, painted 1838, Turner, Joseph Mallord William (1775-1851)/National Gallery, London, UK/The Bridgeman Art Library